A Note to Parents and Caregivers:

Read-it! Readers are for children who are just starting on the amazing road to reading. These beautiful books support both the acquisition of reading skills and the love of books.

 The PURPLE LEVEL presents basic topics and objects using high frequency words and simple language patterns.

 The RED LEVEL presents familiar topics using common words and repeating sentence patterns.

 The BLUE LEVEL presents new ideas using a larger vocabulary and varied sentence structure.

 The YELLOW LEVEL presents more challenging ideas, a broad vocabulary, and wide variety in sentence structure.

 The GREEN LEVEL presents more complex ideas, an extended vocabulary range, and expanded language structures.

 The ORANGE LEVEL presents a wide range of ideas and concepts using challenging vocabulary and complex language structures.

When sharing a book with your child, read in short stretches, pausing often to talk about the pictures. Have your child turn the pages and point to the pictures and familiar words. And be sure to reread favorite stories or parts of stories.

There is no right or wrong way to share books with children. Find time to read with your child, and pass on the legacy of literacy.

Adria F. Klein, Ph.D.
Professor Emeritus
California State University
San Bernardino, California

Editor: Jill Kalz
Designer: Lori Bye
Page Production: Melissa Kes
Art Director: Nathan Gassman
Associate Managing Editor: Christianne Jones
The illustrations in this book were created with watercolors.

Picture Window Books
151 Good Counsel Drive
P.O. Box 669
Mankato, MN 56002-0669
877-845-8392
www.picturewindowbooks.com

Printed in the United States of America.

All books published by Picture Window Books
are manufactured with paper containing at least
10 percent post-consumer waste.

Library of Congress Cataloging-in-Publication Data
Labairon, Cassandra Sharri.
Marty Marley's mighty mountain / by Cassandra Labairon ; illustrated by
Anna Kaiser.
p. cm. — (Read-it! readers: tongue twisters)
ISBN 978-1-4048-4887-0 (library binding)
[1. Tongue twisters—Fiction. 2. Mountains—Fiction.] I. Kaiser, Anna
(Anna Leigh), 1985- ill. II. Title.
PZ7.L1113Mar 2008
[E]—dc22
                                       2008006331

Marty Marley's Mighty Mountain

by Cassandra Labairon
illustrated by Anna Kaiser

Special thanks to our reading adviser:

Adria F. Klein, Ph.D.
Professor Emeritus, California State University
San Bernardino, California

PICTURE WINDOW BOOKS
Minneapolis, Minnesota

Marty Marley and his family were moving miles away. More than anything, Marty wanted to live near a mighty mountain.

But Marty's mother said, "There aren't many mountains where we're moving, Marty."

When the van stopped, Marty Marley jumped out. His mouth opened wide. Behind the new Marley home was a muddy mound.

"A mountain! A mighty mountain!" Marty cried.

Marty's mother said, "That's not a mountain, Marty. That's a muddy mound!"

But Marty cheered. He thought his new mountain was marvelous.

Marty named his mountain Mount More.

Marty's mountain mattered more than marshmallows. It mattered more than malts. It even mattered more than meatballs.

9

Marty loved his mountain. He sang this melody:

My mountain may not be magic.
It is muddy as can be.
But Marty's Mount More is mighty
and made for me-me-me!

"Marty, stop monkeying around on that mound of mud. Make a new friend," said Marty's mother one day.

So, Marty made friends with Miles Middleton.

Marty showed Miles his mighty mountain. Much to Marty's surprise, Miles said, "You're mad, Marty Marley! That's not a mountain. That's a muddy mound!"

But Marty merely smiled. His mountain mattered more than movies. It mattered more than magic. It even mattered more than money.

Soon Miles Middleton learned to love Mount More, too.

15

Marty and Miles read magazines on Mount More. They made monsters out of the mountain's mud. Miles even learned Marty's melody:

My mountain may not be magic.
It is muddy as can be.
But Marty's Mount More is mighty
and made for me-me-me!

Then one morning, Marty's mother had a terrible message.

"That mound is a mess, Marty," she said. "It must be moved to make room for a maple."

"Mom," Marty moaned. "My mighty mountain must stay! Please, please, not a tree!"

Marty marched off with much on his mind. Soon his mighty mountain would be a memory.

On Monday, Marty heard a mighty machine on
his mountain.

"It's mashing Mount More!" Marty moaned. "My mighty mountain will be nothing but mush!"

When Marty got outside, the machine had stopped. It hadn't moved Marty's mountain.

Marty's mother stood next to the maple on Mount More's muddy top.

"Mom! You saved my mountain!" Marty cried.

Marty's mountain mattered more than muffins. It mattered more than milk. But the mountain didn't matter more than hugs from Marty's mother.

More *Read-it!* Readers

Bright pictures and fun stories help you practice your reading skills. Look for more books at your level.

Alex and the Team Jersey

Alex and Toolie

Another Pet

Betty and Baxter's Batter Battle

The Big Pig

Bliss, Blueberries, and the Butterfly

Camden's Game

Cass the Monkey

Gordon Grizwald's Grumpy Goose

Harold Hickok Had the Hiccups

Kyle's Recess

Lady Lulu Liked to Litter

Marconi the Wizard

Peppy, Patch, and the Bath

Pets on Vacation

The Princess and the Tower

Sausages!

Theodore the Millipede

The Three Princesses

Tromso the Troll

Willie the Whale

The Zoo Band

On the Web

FactHound offers a safe, fun way to find Web sites related to topics in this book. All of the sites on FactHound have been researched by our staff.

1. Visit *www.facthound.com*

2. Type in this special code: 1404848878

3. Click on the FETCH IT button.

Your trusty FactHound will fetch the best sites for you!

A complete list of *Read-it!* Readers is available on our Web site: **www.picturewindowbooks.com**